This book belongs
to

_____

children's
choice®

MR. RABBIT
and the LOVELY PRESENT

by CHARLOTTE ZOLOTOW   *Pictures by* MAURICE SENDAK

HARPER & ROW · PUBLISHERS · NEW YORK AND EVANSTON

A Children's Choice® Book Club Edition From Scholastic Book Services

MR. RABBIT AND THE LOVELY PRESENT

Text copyright © 1962 by Charlotte Zolotow
Pictures copyright © 1962 by Maurice Sendak

Printed in the United States of America
ISBN: 0-590-75752-0

for Buena Dapolonia

"Mr. Rabbit," said the little girl, "I want help."

"Help, little girl, I'll give you help if I can," said Mr. Rabbit.

"Mr. Rabbit," said the little girl, "it's about my mother."

"Your mother?" said Mr. Rabbit.

"It's her birthday," said the little girl.

"Happy birthday to her then," said Mr. Rabbit. "What are you giving her?"

"That's just it," said the little girl. "That's why I want help. I have nothing to give her."

"Nothing to give your mother on her birthday?" said Mr. Rabbit. "Little girl, you really do want help."

"I would like to give her something that she likes," said the little girl.

"Something that she likes is a good present," said Mr. Rabbit.

"But what?" said the little girl.

"Yes, what?" said Mr. Rabbit.

"She likes red," said the little girl.

"Red," said Mr. Rabbit. "You can't give her red."

"Something red, maybe," said the little girl.

"Oh, something red," said Mr. Rabbit.

"What is red?" said the little girl.

"Well," said Mr. Rabbit, "there's red underwear."

"No," said the little girl, "I can't give her that."

"There are red roofs," said Mr. Rabbit.

"No, we have a roof," said the little girl. "I don't want to give her that."

"There are red birds," said Mr. Rabbit, "red cardinals."

"No," said the little girl, "she likes birds in trees."

"There are red fire engines," said Mr. Rabbit.

"No," said the little girl, "she doesn't like fire engines."

"Well," said Mr. Rabbit, "there are apples."

"Good," said the little girl. "That's good. She likes apples.
But I need something else."

"What else does she like?" said Mr. Rabbit.

"Well, she likes yellow," said the little girl.

"Yellow," said Mr. Rabbit. "You can't give her yellow."

"Something yellow, maybe," said the little girl.

"Oh, something yellow," said Mr. Rabbit.

"What is yellow?" said the little girl.

"Well," said Mr. Rabbit, "there are yellow taxicabs."

"I'm sure she doesn't want a taxicab," said the little girl.

"The sun is yellow," said Mr. Rabbit.

"But I can't give her the sun," said the little girl, "though I would if I could."

"A canary bird is yellow," said Mr. Rabbit.

"She likes birds in trees," the little girl said.

"That's right, you told me," said Mr. Rabbit. "Well, butter is yellow. Does she like butter?"

"We have butter," said the little girl.

"Bananas are yellow," said Mr. Rabbit.

"Oh, good. That's good," said the little girl. "She likes bananas. I need something else, though."

"What else does she like?" said Mr. Rabbit.

"She likes green," said the little girl.

"Green," said Mr. Rabbit. "You can't give her green."

"Something green, maybe," said the little girl.

"Emeralds," said the rabbit. "Emeralds make a lovely gift."

"I can't afford an emerald," said the little girl.

"Parrots are green," said Mr. Rabbit, "but she likes birds in trees."

"No," said the little girl, "parrots won't do."

"Peas and spinach," said Mr. Rabbit. "Peas are green. Spinach is green."

"No," said the little girl. "We have those for dinner all the time."

"Caterpillars," said Mr. Rabbit. "Some of them are very green."

"She doesn't care for caterpillars," the little girl said.

"How about pears?" said Mr. Rabbit. "Bartlett pears?"

"The very thing," said the little girl. "That's the very thing. Now I have apples and bananas and pears, but I need something else."

"What else does she like?" said Mr. Rabbit.

"She likes blue," the little girl said.

"Blue. You can't give her blue," said Mr. Rabbit.

"Something blue, maybe," said the little girl.

"Lakes are blue," said the rabbit.

"But I can't give her a lake, you know," said the little girl.

"Stars are blue."

"I can't give her stars," the little girl said, "but I would if I could."

"Sapphires make a lovely gift," said Mr. Rabbit.

"But I can't afford sapphires, either," said the little girl.

"Bluebirds are blue, but she likes birds in trees," said Mr. Rabbit.

"Right," said the little girl.

"How about blue grapes?" said Mr. Rabbit.

"Yes," said the little girl. "That is good, very good. She likes grapes. Now I have apples and pears and bananas and grapes."

"That makes a good gift," said Mr. Rabbit. "All you need now is a basket."

"I have a basket," said the little girl.

So she took her basket and she filled it with the green pears and the yellow bananas and the red apples and the blue grapes. It made a lovely present.

"Thank you for your help, Mr. Rabbit," said the little girl.

"Not at all," said Mr. Rabbit. "Very glad to help."

"Good-by, now," said the little girl.

"Good-by," said Mr. Rabbit, "and a happy birthday and a happy basket of fruit to your mother."

The End

Look Who's Part of the Children's Choice® Family!

Something special for
Children's Choice® Book Club members

You can get all these storybook favorites—Puss in Boots, Babar, Curious George, Lyle, George and Martha and The Year at Maple Hill Farm—to hang up on your wall. They're big (17″ × 22″) and beautiful posters, printed in full color on high quality paper. Best of all, you can get all 6 for just $3.95, including postage and handling.

Please allow 3-6 weeks for delivery. Your posters are mailed in a tube, so they won't be creased at all.

Offer expires December 31, 1980

To order your set of 6 Children's Choice® posters, please send your name, address and $3.95 in check or money order to:

**CHILDREN'S CHOICE®
POSTERS
2931 East McCarty St.
P.O. Box 1068
Jefferson City, Mo. 65102**